For Dominik, with love

Simon the sheep

This is Simon. Simon is a sheep. It's eight o'clock. Simon is on his way to school.

MUH

Simon has got a problem. His eyes are not very good. He can't see very well. In school, he sits in the last row. He can't see what the teacher is writing on the board.

home

And he can't see his friends when they talk to him. "Hey Simon, how are you?" someone shouts. "Hm," Simon thinks. Is that his friend Joe? Or Willy?

8AK

One day, his mother takes him to the doctor. "Read the numbers!" the old doctor says to Simon. Simon looks at the numbers. The big ones are easy: Five, seven, three. But Simon can't read the small numbers. Is it a nine? Or a seven? Three or zero?

Y

"Your son needs glasses!" the doctor says to Simon's mother. "With the glasses Simon will see better in school."

Oh no! Simon is shocked. He doesn't like the glasses. "With the glasses, I look like an idiot!" he thinks. "What will my friends at school say? And I can't play in the football team any more with glasses!"

SHEEPSCH

The next day at school all the other sheep laugh at him. "Simon the blind sheep with the glasses!" they shout. Simon is sad. He cries. You can see tears on his face.

SHEEP SCHOOL

Simon is sitting under a tree in front of the school.
Lucy, a pretty sheep girl comes up to him: "What's wrong with you, Simon? Why are you crying?"
Simon tells her his story. Lucy listens to him. Then she puts her arm around Simon. "I like your glasses," she says, "because I like you. Do you want to go to the school party with me tomorrow?"
Simon is happy. Lucy wants to go to the school party with HIM!

YOU CAN'T JUDGE A BOOK BY LOOKING AT ITS COVER...
SHEEP PARTY TONIC

Simon's friends are shocked. Lucy, the prettiest girl in the school comes with Simon!
The party is really cool and the music is good. Simon and Lucy dance and have lots of fun.